by Anna Kang *illustrated by* Christopher Weyant

It Is
(Not) Perfect

Published by Two Lions, New York
www.apub.com
Amazon, the Amazon logo, and Two Lions are trademarks of Amazon.com, Inc., or its affiliates.

ISBN-13: 9781542016629
ISBN-10: 1542016622

The illustrations are rendered in ink and watercolor with brush pens on Arches paper.
Book design by Abby Dening

Printed in China
First Edition
1 3 5 7 9 10 8 6 4 2

two lions

PAT
PAT
PAT

In loving memory of
Drs. Edward K. Kang and David M.Williams,
who devoted their lives to
learning, listening, and healing others.

It is perfect!

And it needs
arches.

And windows.

SNOW CONES

PLOINK!

SMILE!